DON'T BELIEVE A WORD

DON'T BELIEVE A WORD

A WORD

Patricia MacDonald

This first world edition published 2016
in Great Britain and the USA by
SEVERN HOUSE PUBLISHERS LTD of
19 Cedar Road, Sutton, Surrey, England, SM2 5DA.
Trade paperback edition first published
in Great Britain and the USA 2016 by
SEVERN HOUSE PUBLISHERS LTD

British Library Cataloguing in Publication Data

MacDonald, Patricia J. author.
  Don't believe a word.
  1. Mothers and daughters–Fiction. 2. Murder–
  Investigation–Fiction. 3. Suspense fiction.
  I. Title
  813.6-dc23

ISBN-13: 978-0-7278-8587-6 (cased)
ISBN-13: 978-1-84751-686-2 (trade paper)
ISBN-13: 978-1-78010-750-9 (e-book)

Typeset by Palimpsest Book Production Ltd.,
Falkirk, Stirlingshire, Scotland.

DON'T BELIEVE A WORD

Patricia MacDonald

This first world edition published 2016
in Great Britain and the USA by
SEVERN HOUSE PUBLISHERS LTD of
19 Cedar Road, Sutton, Surrey, England, SM2 5DA.
Trade paperback edition first published
in Great Britain and the USA 2016 by
SEVERN HOUSE PUBLISHERS LTD

British Library Cataloguing in Publication Data

MacDonald, Patricia J. author.
  Don't believe a word.
  1. Mothers and daughters–Fiction. 2. Murder–
  Investigation–Fiction. 3. Suspense fiction.
  I. Title
  813.6-dc23

ISBN-13: 978-0-7278-8587-6 (cased)
ISBN-13: 978-1-84751-686-2 (trade paper)
ISBN-13: 978-1-78010-750-9 (e-book)

Typeset by Palimpsest Book Production Ltd.,
Falkirk, Stirlingshire, Scotland.

To my agent and friend, Meg Ruley,
for her charm and cheer, insight and integrity.
I can never thank you enough.

ACKNOWLEDGEMENTS

I am blessed with extraordinary agents and publishers at home and abroad. Special thanks to Peggy Boulos-Smith and her compatriots at JRA in NYC, Edwin Buckhalter and Kate Lyall Grant at Severn House in London, and Catherine LaPautre and Anne Michel in Paris. My deepest gratitude to my publisher at Albin Michel, Francis Esminard, who understood me, even though my French was incomprehensible. And a wistful au revoir to the incomparable Danielle Boesflug.

ONE

Eden Radley raised her collar and pulled her jacket tightly around herself as she picked her way along the icy sidewalk on the Brooklyn street where she lived. She had a wool scarf wrapped high around her neck, but her nose and cheeks were stinging in the chilly night air. She glanced ahead and saw golden light from inside the Brisbane Tavern spilling out onto the sidewalk. She hurried toward the door, eager to slip into the warmth.

Normally her favorite watering hole was the bar in the Black Cat Restaurant, across from her apartment, but it was Sunday night, the Giants were playing a night game, and Eden had heard that they showed the Giants games on several large TV screens in the Brisbane. At least, if this date was a bust, she could keep an eye on the score. Judging from her past internet dating experience, she didn't expect to be here for very long. Just a drink or two, and then she planned to watch the second half alone, in her apartment, preferably under the covers.

Eden had had over a dozen dates since she joined the online dating service. The guys she met had ranged from weird to merely dull, except for one, a lawyer whom she liked immediately. They had talked for hours, and he seemed positively reluctant to part from her. She went home on a cloud, expecting a text from him any minute to request another date.

Two weeks went by and she didn't hear from him. She finally broke down and texted him, careful to sound casual. 'I thought we had a good time,' she said. 'I was hoping we could do it again some evening.' His reply came back: 'I have a lot on my plate these days. If I have a window, I'll call you.'

A window? Really? she thought. To hell with internet dating. From now on she was going back to hoping against hope that she would meet someone in a normal way. This date with Jake Latham, a chemist working for a drug company, was the last item on her dating service to-do list.

They had agreed to meet at a table in the back of the Brisbane, far from the noisy bar, but it was late in the football season and the Brisbane was packed. A table seemed to be out of the question. Eden scanned the room, trying to spot tonight's prospect from the photos on his profile. Nobody was alone or looking around as if trying to find someone. No Jake Latham. She hesitated by the front door, and then strode up to the bar and hoisted herself on a barstool between two parties of boisterous fans. The bartender, a guy who she reckoned to be in his mid-thirties, his dark hair already shot through with gray, looked at her with raised eyebrows. She asked for a glass of white wine. He wiped off the shining dark wood surface of the bar, poured out a glass of wine and set it in front of her. The delicate wine glass looked lost in the forest of dark green and brown beer bottles which crowded the bar.

'Game night,' he said, almost apologetically.

'I know,' said Eden. 'That's why I'm here.' Ordinarily, she would have felt uncomfortable to be alone, seated on a barstool, but she was a Giants fan, at ease with this group of customers. She looked up at the TV screen and sipped her wine.

''Scuse me,' said a deep voice.

Eden turned to look. The guy was ruddy-faced and looked more like a bobsledder than a chemist. It was not the guy in the profile picture. She smiled at him anyway.

'Mind if I slip in here? I'm with these guys,' he said, pointing to the group next to her.

Eden shook her head. The ruddy-faced guy turned his back on her and high-fived the men to her right. He took no further notice of Eden.

Her face flamed but she continued to watch the game. It's not your fault, she reassured herself. You look good tonight. She examined her reflection between the gleaming bottles on the mirrored back of the mahogany bar. Her long dark hair fell in a shining curve over her shoulders, and her blue-and-raspberry wool scarf was perfect for her pale complexion and rosy cheeks. The bartender, who was facing the mirror, caught her eye and gave her a thumbs up.

Embarrassed, Eden hesitated, and then smiled back. The

bartender served the customer next to her. Then he turned to Eden. 'So, you're a fan,' he said.

She shrugged. 'Yeah. Although I'm actually here to meet someone.'

'A fellow fan?' he asked.

'We'll see,' she said. 'We've never met.'

'Are you from the neighborhood?' he asked.

Eden nodded. 'But the Black Cat is my local.'

'I like their food,' he said. 'Those Thai spring rolls.'

She smiled. 'I know. Me too.'

He nodded and then answered the summons of the next customer.

Eden looked at the clock and glanced back at the door again. All of a sudden she felt her phone vibrate against her hip. She fished for it in her jacket pocket, expecting it to be from Jake, and quickly noted the name of the sender: Tara Darby, her mother. In spite of herself, Eden's temper flared.

'Hi, Eden. Miss you. Can you talk? Call me.'

Oh sure, Eden thought. And tell you about how I am trying to meet a stranger on an internet date? She knew exactly what her mother would think about that. Tara's life was not about stilted, planned meetings. It was about stars colliding. During Eden's childhood, Tara was a stay-at-home mom who worked on the accounts for her husband, Hugh's, masonry business. When Eden was in high school, Tara took a part-time job in a local bookstore that belonged to their neighbors across the street. Tara was in charge of arranging events. She invited a short story writer from New York City, who had grown up in their village of Robbin's Ferry, to do a reading and signing. Flynn Darby was a handsome Harvard grad, thirteen years her junior. The two of them fell hopelessly in love. Tara threw away everything – Eden, her father and their home together – for her grand passion, her destiny.

All their friends and family claimed to find Tara's behavior unforgivable. But beneath the widespread condemnation, Eden often thought she detected a tiny hint of admiration for a woman who would follow her heart so recklessly. At the age of forty-two, Tara even had a baby with Flynn. After that, her careless rapture fell to earth with a thud. The child, Jeremy, now four, suffered from a rare genetic, usually fatal disorder, and the three of them had moved last year to Ohio to be near the Cleveland Clinic, and the one researcher who was concentrating on Jeremy's terrible condition.

While Eden understood that choice intellectually, and was sorry that her frail half-brother had to endure such suffering, it also meant that she almost never saw her mother. And on the rare occasions when she did, Tara was always too distracted to show much interest in Eden's life.

Eden hesitated and then texted her mother back. 'Can't. Watching the game.' She slipped her phone back into her pocket.

That will piss her off, she thought. Sunday afternoons, when Eden was a girl, she used to sit beside her large, gentle father on the sofa, watching the TV, and he would patiently explain what every player did, and why. At first she only pretended to listen. She really didn't care about the game. It was enough that her father enjoyed it, and wanted her company. But by the time his daughter was nine or ten, Hugh Radley had converted her into a hopeless fan. Sunday afternoons in the season, plus the odd Monday, Thursday and Sunday nights, if the Giants were playing, Eden and Hugh were glued to the NFL on TV.

Tara Radley, a classic beauty with long, wavy black hair, often went out to read on the porch of their charming Victorian house in Westchester County, just to escape the roar of the fans, the excited commentary of the announcers, the war whoops or cries of disgust from her husband and daughter. Sometimes, when it was a four o'clock game, Tara would escape for wine and appetizers to a bar in the trendy downtown area of Robbin's Ferry. She would meet her friend, Charlene Harris, a realtor who was divorced, childless, and free on Sundays. Eden and Hugh would breathe a little easier once Tara was on her way, and they could watch in peace. Tara always came home mildly tipsy, but usually in a better mood than when she left.

'I don't know how you can stand to watch football,' Tara said to Eden once, lifting her penetrating, brown-eyed gaze from her book and frowning, perplexed, at her only child, her daughter. 'It's so . . . violent.'

'It's exciting,' Eden had said defensively.

'Grown men knocking each other over to get at a ball,' Tara sniffed.

'Dad likes it,' Eden protested.

'I know,' said Tara, stifling a sigh. 'I don't understand him either.'

At the time, her mother's words had seemed amusing. Tara was a reader and a dreamer, not a football fan. Everyone to their own taste, Hugh Radley always said. Now, looking back on it, Eden saw it differently. Tara's complaint had been a narrow fissure in the rock that was their world, their life together, their family. To Eden, her parents seemed content together. But beneath that placid surface, there were numerous cracks, and they were widening into crevices which would wind up breaking Eden's world apart.

The divorce marked the end of so many things in Eden's life. In order to divide their assets, Hugh was forced to take out a second mortgage on their house and money became extremely tight. Six months after her mother left them, Hugh suffered a heart attack and could not work for several months. Instead of attending Yale, where she had been accepted, Eden enrolled as a commuter at Mt St Vincent's in the Bronx, and commuted from home. She had no social life at college. It was all she could juggle to attend her classes, work in the library and rush home to her father. In the ensuing years, he often told her how guilty he felt that she had missed out on so much of college life in order to stay with him, and help him recover.

It doesn't matter, she always replied. What she actually meant was, it wasn't your fault. You weren't the one to blame.

'Hear from your friend?' the bartender shouted amiably above the din.

Eden shook her head. 'He's late.' She looked at the clock again. It was nearly eight-thirty. 'Very late. And he hasn't called.'

'Check your messages again,' he suggested. 'You can't hear anything with the racket in here.'

Eden nodded, realizing that this was true, and pulled out her iPhone again. Sure enough, she had missed a call. She tried to listen to the voicemail, but it was a broken, garbled message, indecipherable in the noisy bar.

She was getting ready to text him. To explain that she couldn't hear the message. To ask why he was late. She was starting to key it in, and then she hesitated. Why bother? she thought. If she were honest with herself, she was actually relieved that he hadn't shown up. She had waited a sufficient amount of time, and she was off the hook. Why not just ignore it and go home?

She considered it for a moment, but she had been raised to be more courteous than that. *Can't hear your voicemail*, she texted. *Where are you?*

She waited for a few minutes, and finally he replied. *Traffic at a standstill.*

Eden looked at the message with narrowed eyes. Was this real, or an excuse? That was the problem with dating a complete stranger. How were you supposed to know? *Let's do this another time*, she wrote, and sent it.

'Did you get him?' asked the bartender, holding the bottle of wine tilted over her empty glass.

Eden shook her head and covered the glass with her palm. 'No, I'm going to go,' she said.

'Stay a while. Game's just starting.' He had a sad-eyed smile and was good-looking, sturdy but trim. Probably an actor, or a would-be writer, she thought, bartending to make ends meet, like most of her friends in the neighborhood.

She smiled in reply. 'No, I can't. But thanks.' She stuffed her phone resolutely back in her pocket, and pulled out her credit card, handing it to him.

He glanced at the name on the card and then handed it back to her, shaking his head. 'It's on the house, Eden,' he said.

Eden was taken aback. She wondered if he routinely bought drinks for the girls who were stood up on his shift. Perhaps that was considered good public relations at the Brisbane. 'Oh. Well. Thanks. That's nice of you.'

'Vince Silver,' he said, extending his hand across the bar.

Eden took it and shook it. 'Thanks, Vince.'

'Maybe I'll see you in the Black Cat,' he said.

She smiled and nodded, slipping off the barstool. She could hardly wait to get out of the Brisbane Tavern. She would watch the game from her own comfortable sofa. She pulled on her coat and edged her way through the crowd, as an excited fan quickly slipped in behind her and settled himself on her vacated stool.

The game ran into overtime, and it was past midnight before it was over. Eden's eyelids were heavy by the time the final kick won the game for Detroit. She thought about calling her father to review the game, but that was never any fun when the Giants lost. Besides, she was too tired. She brushed her teeth, turned off the light and got into bed, expecting to be asleep instantly. But the constant exchange of the lead in the game had invaded her head. She tossed and turned for over an hour before sleep overtook her.

The next morning she was groggy on the train to Manhattan, but she felt a bit more awake by the time she had walked from the subway stop to the offices of DeLaurier Publishing. She had worked for the publisher for four years, and she had recently been promoted to the position of Associate Editor, with a small office all her own. Eden greeted the editorial assistants whom she passed in the hallway with a hail of 'Good morning' and 'How was your weekend?'

'Looks like you had a rough one,' observed Gillian Munroe, a roving assistant who worked for Eden as well as two other editors.

Eden shrugged. She was not fooling anyone. 'I wish I could tell you I was doing something exciting. But I couldn't sleep after watching the Giants game.'

Gillian grimaced. 'Football?'

'Absolutely,' said Eden.

'Whatever floats your boat.' Gillian was only twenty-two, and had a peachy complexion which no amount of sleeplessness could dim. Eden thought that twenty-two seemed like a lifetime ago, although in truth she was only twenty-seven herself. But sometimes Gillian made her feel a little bit . . . past her prime.

Don't forget, she reminded herself, Gillian works for you. She'd love to be in your shoes. Eden was pleased with her progress at DeLaurier Publishing. She was on the editorial fast track. The editorial director, Rob Newsome, was already including her in new, high-level projects, encouraging her ambition. All in all, Eden reminded herself, as she poured a cup of coffee and picked up a muffin in the break room, she was doing pretty well. She took her breakfast back to her office and sat down to eat it at her desk. It was a morning ritual she thoroughly enjoyed.

When she went to college, Eden's dream was to get her degree and move to New York City so she could become part of the publishing industry. In this one way, she had been more like her mother, always gravitating to books and literature. Of course, unlike her mother, she reminded herself, she had made her dream come true. She was actually working with authors on the publication of books, not just daydreaming and selling a few copies in a bookstore.

'Hey,' said a friendly voice.

Eden put down her coffee cup and looked up. Sophy McKay, a senior editor, stood in the doorway, tapping on the open door.

'Come on in,' Eden said, indicating a chair.

Sophy came in and slid into the chair in front of Eden's desk. 'So . . . how was your weekend?' she said suggestively.

Eden shook her head. Sophy had met her husband on match.com, and was a tireless proselytizer for the benefits of internet dating. Sometimes Eden wondered if it wasn't a case of misery loving company. 'It was fine,' she said.

'So. Spill. You had a date?'

'I had a date,' Eden said. 'But he didn't show up.'

Sophy frowned. 'I'm sorry.'

Eden shrugged. 'No big deal. I met a nice bartender while I was waiting.'

'A bartender? Eden, you're trying to meet a professional.'

'No, I'm not,' said Eden evenly.

'Did you see your dad this weekend?' Sophy asked.

Eden knew that this question was a trap. Sophy made no effort to disguise her opinion that Eden spent too much time worrying about her father. She shook her head. 'My dad went to a *Beef and Beer* for some guy he used to work with. I think he took our neighbor across the street.'

'Ah, chasing after the ladies, is he?'

Eden laughed. 'Hardly,' she said. 'They're old friends.' Gerri Zerbo, who, with her husband, had owned the bookstore where Tara had fatefully gone to work, was recently widowed. Magnus had been ill for several years before his death from lung disease, and they had been forced to close the bookstore. Now, despite having two grown children – a son and a daughter, who were married with children and lived nearby – Gerri found her new, unwanted status to be lonely. Hugh sometimes invited her to events he thought she might enjoy.

'Maybe there's more to it than that,' said Sophy. 'You never know.'

Eden shook her head. 'Trust me.' For as long as she could remember, Gerri and Magnus had been a fixture in their lives. Gerri was more shocked and dismayed than almost anyone when Tara ran off with her short story writer. Part of her felt guilty for having offered Tara the job at the bookstore which led, ultimately, to Hugh and Tara's breakup. 'Your mom and dad had a good marriage,' Gerri often said, shaking her head as she dropped off a plate of cookies, or drove Eden to the train station when her dad was working. 'What was she thinking? I will never understand it.'

'How was your weekend?' Eden asked politely.

Sophy ticked it off on her fingers. 'Holiday dance recital. Dinner at Jim's parents' house 'cause his younger brother is home from India . . .'

As Sophy recounted her busy domestic life, Eden's attention wandered. She glanced at the homepage on her desktop. The usual headlines with photos were on display for a moment, and then they were replaced by the next tragedy. 'Murder/ Suicide in Cleveland, Ohio.' Cleveland, Eden thought with a shiver. That's where her mother lived. 'Police in Cleveland, Ohio have reason to believe that a mother killed herself and her severely disabled young son by carbon monoxide poisoning . . .' Eden glanced at the house on the screen, surrounded by snow. She had never been to visit Tara in Ohio. But she had seen photos on Facebook of Tara with her new family, in front of their house. It was a small, relatively new house painted French blue, like the house on the screen. Gooseflesh rose on her arms.

'. . . and I had to bake cupcakes for Jenny's preschool. Eden, are you listening?'

Eden shook her head.

Sophy frowned. 'What's the matter? You look white as a ghost.'

'This headline,' Eden muttered.

'What about it?' Sophy asked.

'It sounds like . . . But it couldn't be.'

Sophy frowned. 'What happened?'

Eden shook her head. 'A woman and her son. They're saying it was a murder/suicide.'

'So?' said Sophy.

'My mother lives in Cleveland. The house in the video. It looks just like my mother's house. Their house is that same French blue.'

'Oh, Eden. The colors are always distorted on those videos. Besides, I'm sure you would have heard something . . .'

Eden ignored her, scrolling through the article, as sweat broke out on her forehead and under her arms. Details were scant. They were withholding names until the next of kin could be contacted.

Just then, the phone rang on Eden's desk. She picked it up.

'Eden Radley,' she said.

'This is Melissa in reception. Your father is here to see you.'

Instantly, Eden's hands began to shake. She knew. 'I'll be right out,' she whispered.

She stood up, brushing off the muffin crumbs from her shirt. 'My father is here,' she said to Sophy. Her legs felt stiff as she stood up. It was difficult to move.

Sophy looked worried. 'Do you want me to come with you?'

Eden shook her head. She went down the hall and out the doors to the reception area. Melissa sat alone at a large desk beneath the DeLaurier logo. She inclined her head toward the comfortable furniture grouping in the corner.

A man stood up from his chair. Hugh Radley was a tall man, as wide as those Giant linebackers whom he admired so much. Even though he was balding, and slightly too thick around the middle, Eden always thought her father was handsome. He had even features, keen eyes, and he exuded a quiet authority. He was solid, but not suave, even under the best of circumstances. He rarely came to New York. He found Manhattan baffling. Eden saw the look in his eyes, and her knees felt as if they would buckle beneath her.

'Dad . . .' she whispered.

'I didn't want you to hear this on the phone,' he said.

Eden tried to speak, but she could not form the words. 'What is it . . .' she managed to croak.

Hugh's face was pale and grim. 'I've just had a call from the Cleveland police.'

Eden's heart lurched. She felt her world crumbling into pieces again, the way it had nine years ago, when her mother announced that she was leaving them to remarry. 'What happened?'

Hugh gave a shaky sigh. 'Sweetie, I'm so sorry. It's your mother. And your half-brother, Jeremy. They were found this morning. Dead. In the house.'

'It was online. I saw it was Cleveland, I had a bad feeling . . .'

Hugh shook his head sadly. 'Carbon monoxide poisoning.'

'They called it a murder/suicide.'

'I wish they'd stop saying that,' Hugh said angrily.

Eden was trembling all over. 'She just texted me last night.'

'Your mom? What did she want?' Hugh asked.

'To talk,' Eden whispered. Was it possible that her mother was considering the most terrible deed imaginable and called her for help? Eden shook her head. That simmering anger which she frequently felt toward her mother was like a crutch. A crutch which had now been unceremoniously kicked out of her reach.

'I thought you might want to come home with me,' said Hugh. 'It's such a shock. You can't possibly stay at work. I know I couldn't.'

Eden was thinking about that text. Watching the game, she had said. You can wait, was the subliminal message, until I'm damn good and ready. She had enjoyed defying her request to talk. Now, they would never talk again.

Melissa, the receptionist, came tiptoeing up to them, her

face at once concerned and apologetic. 'Can I help? Is there anything . . .?'

'My daughter's things,' said Hugh. 'Her pocketbook and such. They're probably in her office. Could you go and get them for us? I'm taking Eden home. We've had a death in the family.'

'Sure,' said Melissa. 'Oh, Eden, I'm so sorry. I'll be right back.' She hurried past her own desk and pushed open the door to the editorial offices.

Hugh had his arm around Eden, supporting her. She was reminded of the days after his heart attack when he would lean on her in order to walk. It had been quite a while since she needed to lean on him. 'Take it easy,' Hugh said. 'I'll get you home and you can rest.'

Eden shook her head as a tear streaked down her cheek. 'I said no to Mom. I wouldn't talk to her.'

'Oh, sweetie,' said Hugh. 'Don't beat yourself up over it. You didn't know . . .'

'I should have talked to her.'

'This is not your fault. None of this,' Hugh said firmly.

But Eden was not looking for consolation. She was miles away. Thinking about the small, cookie-cutter-style house she had seen on the screen, where Tara had lived with her boyish husband and their son. 'Where was he?' she demanded.

Hugh frowned. 'You mean . . .'

Eden turned and looked straight into her father's sad eyes. 'Yes. Flynn. Where was he when it happened? Is he dead too?'

Hugh hesitated, and shook his head. 'No. He wasn't there. I don't know why. I don't know all the details.'

Eden felt a sudden fury flash through her like an electric shock. 'He wasn't there?' she asked. 'How lucky for him!'

'Eden, his wife and child are gone,' Hugh admonished her gently. 'I wouldn't call that lucky. He's lost his family.'

Eden's eyes suddenly filled with tears, but not for Flynn Darby. For herself. For her own mother, who had once been the glowing center of her world. 'Now he knows how we felt,' she whispered.

TWO

Hugh drove home, his grim gaze fixed on the road, while Eden shivered, blanketed with both his coat and her own, in the seat beside him. The crowded buildings of the Bronx gave way to the scenic towns and villages of Westchester County. The town of Robbin's Ferry was a mere twenty miles from New York City, but it might have been a thousand miles away. There were plentiful trees and parks, and old houses in the village which had been beautifully, elegantly restored. Robbin's Ferry, a working-class suburb when Eden's parents grew up there, had become, over the years, a high-end place to live. Now, real estate prices were sky high, and most of the old family businesses downtown had given way to sleek furniture and clothing stores, and upscale florists, bakeries, delis and restaurants.

For many, living in Robbin's Ferry was an impossible dream, but for Eden it was just home. She had grown up here and the sight of Robbin's Ferry was always balm to her spirit. Well, not always, she reminded herself. After Tara left them, and Hugh fell ill, home seemed a hollow word for a while. Gradually, over time, it had become dear to her again.

Hugh turned into the driveway and pulled up beside the gray-green gingerbread-style Victorian house with white trim and black shutters. Those colors had been Tara's choice, but Hugh had never wanted to change them. He parked in front of the closed doors of the garage. As soon as he switched off the engine, Gerri Zerbo appeared at her front door across the street, and came outside without a coat. She was middle-aged and doughy, her short, graying hair framing her round face with soft waves, but Eden knew well, it would be a mistake to underestimate her. Gerri had a keen intelligence, and a steely side. Today she opened the door on Eden's side of the car and gazed in at her, her blue eyes brimming with sympathy.

Eden avoided her gaze, unbuckling her seatbelt and handing

her father's coat back to him. Gerri stepped aside so that Eden could get out of the car. Eden pulled her coat tight and slung her purse over her shoulder. Then she met Gerri's gaze.

Gerri shook her head sadly. 'Oh, Eden, I'm so sorry,' she said.

Eden's fragile composure collapsed. She hung her head, and tears began to spill from her eyes. She was gently pulled into Gerri's embrace, and felt a pudgy hand smoothing her hair as Gerri murmured words of comfort. Hugh came around the car, and sighed.

'How are you doing, Hugh?' Gerri asked.

Hugh shook his head. 'Terrible,' he said. 'What a terrible day.'

Gerri gathered herself up briskly. 'Come on,' she said. 'It's freezing out here. Let's go in.'

Eden stumbled up the walkway to the front steps, and followed Gerri into the house. Gerri took Eden's coat and hung it up, while Hugh ushered her into the living room. Eden sank down on one of the faded sofas and pulled a throw over herself.

'I'll be right back,' said Gerri. 'I'm going to get you some snacks.'

'I couldn't eat,' said Eden.

'You never know. You might want something,' said Gerri, disappearing down the hall toward the kitchen.

Hugh sat down on Eden's right in his well-worn leather club chair, and reached out his hand to her. Eden put her hand in his. They had hardly spoken on the way home, but the understanding between them was, as always, comforting.

'Thanks for coming to get me, Dad,' said Eden, wiping her eyes again with a soggy Kleenex. 'I don't know what I would have done.'

'You never have to worry about that,' said Hugh. 'You know you can always count on me.'

'I know,' said Eden, nodding.

They were silent again for a few moments. Then Eden looked at her father. 'They said on the news that it was a murder/suicide, but I can't believe that. She couldn't have done that to Jeremy on purpose,' she insisted.

'I understand that life with Jeremy was . . . very difficult.'

Eden knew what he was saying. The terrible effects of Katz-Ellison syndrome meant that Jeremy couldn't speak, or walk on his own. His life expectancy was uncertain, but most Katz-Ellison sufferers didn't live past the teenage years. He was prone to angry, inchoate outbursts, lashing out at anyone who tried to soothe him. 'I know. But still,' said Eden.

Gerri's footsteps could be heard on the hardwood floor of the hallway, and then she came in carrying a tray of food. 'Here,' she said, setting it down on the coffee table. 'Have something.'

'Thanks,' Eden whispered, but she looked at the tray as if the sight of it made her feel slightly ill. 'I just keep thinking,' she said, 'that people die all the time of carbon monoxide poisoning. Why would they think that it was deliberate . . .?'

'I don't know all the details,' said Hugh gently.

'But why are they even considering this as a possibility?' Eden cried.

Hugh was calm, but definite. 'I spoke to a police detective this morning. I'm afraid they are quite sure this was not an accident. The detective I spoke to said that your mother closed the house up tight and left the car running in the attached garage. The door connected to the house was left wide open.'

'Maybe she forgot,' Gerri suggested stoutly. 'Sometimes when you come in with a load of groceries, and a kid who's giving you a hard time . . .'

Hugh shook his head. 'Apparently, the carbon monoxide detector had been disabled. The windows in the house were taped shut, and the other doors in the house had towels wedged beneath them to keep the gas from escaping. Barbiturates were found at the scene.'

Eden was silent for a moment, picturing it. Her stomach was churning. 'Did she . . . was there a note?' she asked.

'There was,' said her father.

'What did it say?' she demanded.

'They wouldn't tell me that.'

Eden looked helplessly at her father. 'Surely we have a right to know these things.'

Hugh frowned. 'As the detective put it to me, this is a criminal investigation. Maybe when it is over . . .'

'She wouldn't do this,' Eden said stubbornly. Then she faltered. 'I just don't think she would . . .'

There was a silence during which Hugh refrained from pointing out that, all the same, she did, indeed, do this. Eden drew in a breath. 'Where was he?'

'Who?' her father asked patiently.

'Flynn Darby.'

'Apparently he was away somewhere. He found them when he came home this morning.'

Eden glared at him. 'But if she was suicidal, he must have known that. Why didn't he try to get her help? Why wasn't he with them that night? Where was he? Out on the town?'

'I don't know the answer to that, darling,' said Hugh. 'Your mother probably planned this for a night when she knew he would be away. She must have wanted to spare his life.'

Eden stared down at her hands, feeling numb. She could still remember, as if it were yesterday, sitting in the front seat of the car with her mother while Tara tried to explain to her why she was going to leave them to marry Flynn Darby. 'All I can tell you is that I can't imagine life without him. He's my soulmate,' Tara had said. Furious, Eden had gotten out of the car and slammed the door shut, trying to drown out her mother's explanation. What am I? she had wondered then as she turned her back and walked away. What is Dad?

'Yes,' said Eden sullenly. 'Yes, I'm sure you're right.'

Eden felt guilty for missing work, but that evening, when she called her editorial director, Rob Newsome, he told her not to worry. She needed time to make arrangements, and time to process the shock of it all. Take the rest of the week, he said. Eden did not need much convincing.

The next day she was too numb to get dressed. She stayed in her pajamas and surfed the net addictively for any additional information, even though the reports inevitably upset her. In one account the neighbors said that they never saw Jeremy out playing like the other children. He had been seen shrieking and flailing his fists at his mother, though she never raised her voice to him. Neighbors described Flynn Darby as someone who kept to himself, and Tara as an attentive mother. Everyone insisted that there was no other sign of trouble in that house. Day turned into night as Eden searched for explanations. Finally, that evening, on the *Cleveland Plain Dealer* website, an elderly couple who lived next door to the Darbys answered at least one of Eden's nagging questions.

'I heard the boy screaming bloody murder one time, and his mother came over and asked to borrow a stepladder,' said the old man. 'She told me, "The carbon monoxide alarm is too sensitive. It's always going off without warning. My son can't bear the sound of it."

'Her husband wasn't home, so I said I'd help her. I brought over the ladder and took the batteries out.' The old man sighed. 'I told her she should replace it with a new alarm and she said she would. But I guess they didn't.'

Eden's fitful sleep that night was filled with nightmares, and the next morning she was groggy when she was awakened by her father shaking her gently.

'You have a phone call,' he said, indicating the landline extension in her room.

Eden blinked away sleep and felt a pounding in her head as she peered at him. 'Who is it?' she asked.

'Your mother's husband. You need to speak to him.'

Eden was dumbstruck for a moment. Then she sat up, holding the covers around her, and picked up the phone. 'This is Eden,' she said.

'Eden,' said a thick, unfamiliar voice, 'this is Flynn Darby.'

'Oh. Hello,' she said.

'I'm sure you know why I'm calling.'

For a moment, Eden did not reply.

'I'm making funeral arrangements for Friday,' he said. 'Is that convenient for you?'

'Uh yes, I suppose,' she said.

'Yes or no?' he said brusquely.

'Yes,' said Eden.

'Is there anything you want included?'

'I don't know what you mean. Like what?' Eden asked.

'Music. A poem?'

'Offhand, I can't think of anything. All I keep thinking is that I wish it wasn't happening.'

There was a silence from Flynn's end of the line.

Eden forced herself to concentrate. 'I have to say . . . I'm sorry for your loss. Of my mother. And your son.'

'Thanks,' said Flynn brusquely. 'They are having a joint service – Tara and Jeremy. I'll email you all the details.'

'Okay,' said Eden quickly.

'Can you call Tara's sister, Jodie? That would be helpful.'

Eden felt numb. 'Yes. I'll take care of it. I'll call her,' she said. 'Are your . . . um . . . grandparents coming?' she asked. She knew from her mother that the elderly couple lived in Robbin's Ferry where they had raised Flynn after his mother's death. 'I mean, if they . . . you know . . . need a ride to the airport or something . . .'

'That's very nice of you,' said Flynn. 'But my grandmother's in bad health. They're pretty frail, the two of them. They can't make the trip.'

'Oh, I just thought . . . if they needed a ride . . .'

'Thanks. It's just not gonna happen.' There was a silence. Then Flynn said, 'Please tell your father, if he wants to come, he can.'

Eden stiffened. She realized that Flynn was being generous, but still, his suggestion seemed vaguely insulting. 'I'll tell him,' she said.

'Anyone I've forgotten?' he asked.

If Tara and Hugh had never parted, if the funeral were here, in Robbin's Ferry, there would be dozens of people. But now . . . 'No,' said Eden. 'Actually, I'll let Mom's friend, Charlene, know.'

'Okay,' he said abruptly.

Eden could tell that he was about to end the call. 'Wait,' she said. She was silent for a moment.

Flynn sighed.

'Why did she do it?' Eden said.

Flynn was silent for a long moment. Eden thought he might have hung up. 'I'm sure she had her reasons,' he said.

THREE

E den called her Aunt Jodie, and they decided to fly out and meet in Cleveland. Jodie, Tara's younger sister, was a physics professor at Georgia-Tech, and Eden had heard, from those who knew them as children, that Tara was always known as the pretty one, and Jodie as the smart one. Jodie planned to fly from Hartsfield-Jackson in Atlanta. Eden was leaving from Westchester. The two agreed on a time to rendezvous at Cleveland Airport on the morning of the funeral, and they booked hotel rooms near the airport for that night.

Eden had not seen her aunt or her uncle in quite a while. Jodie's husband, Kent, was a journalist, on assignment in the Middle East. Their son, Ben, was in graduate school in California. Eden had fond memories of them at family gatherings when she was a girl, but once Tara married Flynn and gave birth to Jeremy, the family get-togethers stopped happening. Eden was glad to know that Jodie would be with her on this difficult occasion.

When Friday came, Hugh drove Eden to Westchester Airport. He embraced her at the curb outside the terminal. Eden could feel him trembling, and when he pulled away, she saw tears in his eyes. Hugh wiped them away, embarrassed. 'I thought about coming with you. I wish I could be there in a way.'

'Flynn said you were welcome to come,' said Eden. 'I probably should have mentioned it. But I didn't think . . .'

Hugh shook his head. 'No. I wouldn't have come anyway. It's better if I stay away. They had their own life.'

Eden's heart shriveled inside her, thinking about the truth of that statement. Their life with Tara had long been over. 'I probably shouldn't go either. It's not as if they wanted anything to do with me.'

Hugh gave her a warning look. 'It's your mother,' he said. 'She loved you.'

'I know, I know,' she said. 'I'm going.' She hugged him again. 'I better get on that plane.'

He waved as she entered the terminal, and kept waving till she was out of sight.

Jodie beamed at Eden when she saw her at the terminal in Cleveland. 'You look wonderful, Eden,' Jodie exclaimed, hugging her. Even though she was over forty, Jodie wore her hair as she always had, in bangs and a ponytail. It was true that she was not a beauty like Tara, but she had a certain calm self-assurance which her older sister had never possessed.

Eden hugged her back. 'So do you,' she said sincerely. She was so glad to see Jodie's familiar face in this place where she felt ill at ease.

'How was your flight?' Jodie asked.

'Bumpy, but not too long,' said Eden. 'Yours?'

'About the same. Oh, it's good to see you again,' said Jodie. 'I just wish this wasn't the reason . . .'

'Me too,' said Eden.

'I'm so sorry about your mother. We didn't talk that much, but when we did, she always talked about you. She adored you, you know.'

Eden shrugged. 'Not enough, I guess,' she said.

Jodie frowned. 'Don't say that. Whatever made her do this, it wasn't for a lack of love for you. I wish I knew why, but Tara wasn't one to share her problems. In fact, she could be very . . . secretive. I had no idea.' Jodie shook her head.

She tried to call me on the night she died, Eden thought. And I blew her off. She did not mention this to her aunt, but focused on arrangements instead. 'We'll pick up the hotel shuttle,' she said. 'I reserved us a rental car, at the hotel. We can drop our bags off, and then we probably should be on our way.'

'I guess there's no avoiding it,' agreed Jodie grimly.

The day was cold and brilliantly bright. Thanks to the GPS, Eden and her aunt found their way to the funeral home with no difficulty. Eden felt slightly sick as they entered the gloomy sandstone building in downtown Cleveland where the service would be. A large information board in the foyer listed the various visitations which were scheduled. There was no mention of Tara and Jeremy.

Eden went up to one of the undertaking staff. 'Excuse me, are we in the right place? My mother and my half-brother's service is this morning and it's not posted . . .'

'I'm sorry but this funeral is invitation only. I need to have your name,' said the balding, dark-suited man in a hushed tone. He looked around, as if to be sure that there was no one listening.

'Eden Radley,' she said. 'And this is Mrs Jodie Altman.'

The man frowned over a clipboard he was holding, and crossed off a couple of lines. Then he directed them to a room that was tucked away near the back of the first floor. It was a square room wallpapered in a silver stripe, with gray velvet drapes at the windows. It had been set up with chairs for the mourners. At the front of the room were two plain, pine coffins, side by side, both closed. Behind the coffins, on an easel, was a blown-up photo of Tara and Jeremy. The photo had been taken in a field, on a summer day. There was a verdant line of trees at the horizon, and the blue flash of a lake. Tara, wearing a white, gauzy shirt, was sitting in tall grass, surrounded by yellow wildflowers, smiling into the camera, her black hair escaping a messy updo, her brown eyes sad and limpid. She held her arms protectively around Jeremy, her chin resting on the top of his head. The boy had delicate features and shiny hair, but his mouth hung open in a twisted grimace and his eyes were obscured by thick glasses which sat crookedly on his face.

Eden's eyes filled with tears. She looked away.

'It's a beautiful photo,' said Jodie, shaking her head. 'I don't know how she could have done it. Taken the child's life too. I know she adored him.'

Eden nodded and wiped her eyes. 'It just seems so unlike her.'

Jodie stifled a sob, and shook her head.

'Should we sit?' Eden asked, feeling suddenly young and uncertain.

'Well,' said Jodie, 'normally, we'd go and speak to the grieving husband. But I don't see him anywhere. Do you?'

Eden looked around, puzzled. 'No. I don't.'

Just then, a pale young woman with shiny, shoulder-length brown hair and narrow, black-framed glasses approached them. She had waxy, ivory-colored skin, and she seemed lit from within, like a tapered candle. She was dressed in a dark, hipster outfit with a black pea coat, black tights and a short, lacy skirt. A handsome young black man, slim and also bespectacled, with a shaved head of perfect proportions, shadowed her protectively. Unlike most of the men in the room, he was dressed in a suit and tie.

'Are you Eden?' the young woman asked hesitantly.

Eden nodded.

The girl exhaled, and gripped Eden's hand between her lacy, fingerless black gloves. 'I thought so. Your mother always talked about you. My name is Lizzy Jacquez. I'm a grad student in psychology. I do research for Dr Tanaka. I worked closely with Jeremy and your mother. This is my husband, DeShaun Jacquez. Dr Jacquez,' she corrected herself proudly.

The young man smiled. His teeth were perfection. 'She always says that,' he demurred. 'I'm still an intern. Nice to meet you.' He shook Eden's hand in a strong grip.

'I'm so sorry,' Lizzy said. 'Your mother was a wonderful woman. And Jeremy. He was the best boy in the world.'

Then, Eden realized that she had heard Tara mention this girl's name before. 'Oh yes. My mother said that you were a great support to her,' she said.

Lizzy covered her face with her hands. DeShaun put an arm around her. 'You okay, babe?' he murmured.

Lizzy straightened up and took a deep breath. She lifted her glasses with the back of her hand and wiped her eyes. 'I'm supposed to remain objective. Not get involved, but . . .'

'Don't blame yourself for that,' said Eden gently. 'It's only human. By the way, this is my mother's sister, Jodie.' Everyone shook hands.

'I admire the work that you do,' said Jodie. 'It must take a terrible toll on you to work with kids that have such dreadful conditions. And no real hope.'

Lizzy's face brightened with the shining faith of a true

believer. 'Dr Tanaka is determined to discover the treatment that will help these children. They and their families all suffer so much. If anybody can do it, it's him. I lost my own brother, Anthony, to this disease when he was five. I decided right then and there to make it my life's work.'

'That's impressive,' said Eden.

'It's hard to explain, but, if you've been through it, you're really a part of this community. My mother volunteered as a babysitter for Jeremy, just so that Tara and Flynn could get away out once in a while. She and my dad know better than anyone how tough it is to have a child with Katz-Ellison.'

'I'm so sorry,' said Eden. 'Obviously, my mother was surrounded by a lot of very kind people.' She looked around the room, which was slowly filling up. 'Lizzy, do you know where Mr Darby is? I thought he would be right up front.'

Lizzy's eyes welled up again. 'Oh, I'm sure he is so distraught. I don't know where he'll find the strength to face this day.'

Just then, a sturdy, serious-looking Asian man of about fifty, wearing a topcoat, entered the room and looked around. A murmur went up among the mourners, and a cluster of people gathered around him. He nodded toward each of them and then he eased into a seat at the back. Eden suspected that this must be Dr Tanaka, the researcher heading the Katz-Ellison study at the Cleveland Clinic. Her suspicion was confirmed when Lizzy spotted him. 'Dr Tanaka has arrived,' she said in a hushed tone of respect. She turned to DeShaun, who said that he was right behind her, and then she rushed to greet her boss and mentor. Dr Tanaka nodded, and folded his hands. His manner was respectful, but it seemed as if he wished to keep his fellow mourners at arm's length. He showed little other emotion.

'You know, this is just rude,' Jodie fumed. 'I don't care how upset he is. Everybody here is upset. He should be here. Why even have this service if you're not going to show up?'

Eden did not have to ask whom she was referring to. 'I'm sure he intends to show up,' she said.

One of the couples who had hurried to greet Dr Tanaka conferred with each other and then hesitantly approached Eden.

She recognized the well-meaning, uneasy expression on their faces. The woman was slim with an olive complexion and dark curly hair cut in a fashionable bob. She had a beautiful printed scarf draped around her neck. The man had dark hair, a mustache and lively brown eyes.

'Excuse me,' said the woman. 'I saw you talking to Lizzy. Are you Eden?'

Eden nodded.

The woman reached out for her hand. 'My name is Marguerite, and this is my husband, Gerard. I met your mom at the clinic. Our youngest daughter suffers from Katz-Ellison. In fact, a lot of these people are from the clinic. We try our best to support one another.'

'So I understand. It's nice to meet you,' said Eden. 'I'm glad to know my mom had friends here.'

'Well,' said Marguerite. 'She was a beautiful person. She and I kind of bonded over the kids at first. But then we got talking one day and realized that both of us were older than our husbands . . .'

Gerard looked at her aghast, as if she were sharing some terribly personal secret.

'Well, honey, it's true,' said Marguerite. 'And we're both . . . we both loved to read. We would exchange books. We lived only a few streets apart. It gave us a lot in common.'

'I'm sure that was comforting to her,' said Eden.

'I just feel guilty that I didn't do more to help her. She was so anxious lately but I never dreamed . . . I tried to reassure her that she would get through it. But she was a lot more alone than I am. No matter what, Gerard and I are partners in this. We both work, but Gerard's mother moved here from France when she was widowed. And my whole family is in the area. Your mom had nobody but the people at the clinic. Don't get me wrong. They are wonderful people and they really understand. But there's no substitute for having your own family nearby.'

Marguerite's words made Eden squirm with guilt. She'd known very well that her mother was struggling. Maybe she should have made the effort to come out here and get to know Jeremy. She'd rebuffed every invitation, still hurt by

Tara's abandonment. Why hadn't she tried to get beyond her own anger?

'And she had her husband,' Gerard reminded his wife. His French accent was pronounced, and charming.

Marguerite rolled her eyes. Eden looked from one to the other.

'He tried,' said Gerard stoutly. 'It was hard on him too.'

'Well, no one knows that better than you,' said Marguerite, 'but you don't shirk your responsibilities. You step up.'

'We shouldn't be talking about this right now, chérie,' Gerard admonished her. 'Eden doesn't want to hear this kind of talk.'

In fact, Eden wanted to hear more, but it did seem like the wrong time and place. 'I'm wondering where Flynn might be right now,' she said.

Marguerite shook her head. 'I hate to say it, but this is typical. He was never there for her.'

'Eden, we don't want to detain you,' said Gerard, firmly closing the subject. 'I'm sure you have many people to talk to.'

'Thank you both for coming,' said Eden.

Tears welled in Marguerite's eyes. 'Of course we came. Tara and Jeremy were very dear to us.'

'You know, we have a café downtown called Jaune,' said Gerard.

'It's a mélange of Provençal and Middle Eastern cooking. You should come by while you're here. We'd love to feed you dinner,' said Marguerite. 'On the house.'

Eden nodded and thanked them both, knowing she would be leaving the next day, and would probably never visit their restaurant. She watched them as they went and took a seat near the back among the other families from the clinic. Eden thought that Marguerite and Gerard reminded her of the kind of friends she had in Brooklyn. Young, eclectic, dedicated urbanites full of projects and ideas. When she left this place, she reminded herself, she had a life to go back to. A life far away from all this sadness. The thought of it was steadying. She turned away and looked for her aunt, who was already seated. Eden slipped into the chair beside Jodie. She glanced around the room. People were restless. Some were conversing while others nervously glanced at the door, waiting for some kind of direction. Finally, a member of the funeral home staff approached the lectern, which was surrounded by baskets of gladioli and carnations.

'We're going to begin shortly,' he said. 'We're just waiting for . . .'

'I'm here, I'm here,' bellowed a thick, slurry voice. All eyes turned to the back of the room.

Flynn Darby appeared in the center aisle. He was wearing a long wool topcoat that looked like it had come directly from the thrift shop. Under the coat he had on an oversized, shapeless black turtleneck, jeans and engineer's boots which were unlaced. His unruly hair, which was curly and blond, looked almost stiff with dirt and grease. Eden had seen Flynn Darby before, but only fleetingly. Her mother had invited Eden to their apartment several times when they first were together, but Eden always made an excuse. She refused to sit down to dinner with this man who had torn their lives apart. Still, she had always been curious about him. Now, she gazed at him in disbelief. Beside Flynn, a young woman in a headscarf, a shapeless floor-length dress and a blazer, supported him with one arm. Her eyes were almond-shaped and hazel-colored under sharply defined black brows. She wore no make-up, but her face had a kind of grave beauty.

'Who is that with Flynn?' she whispered to Jodie.

Jodie shook her head. 'Who knows?'

'What's the matter with him?' Eden whispered.

'I'm just guessing,' said Jodie, 'but I'd say he's either drunk or stoned.'

He was still a young man, in his mid-thirties, but his glittering blue eyes had dark circles underneath, and looked unfocused. He was even-featured, with high cheekbones and hollow cheeks. He had a wide, full-lipped mouth, and there was a flash of white teeth as he curled his lip and snarled, 'Whass everybody looking at? I'm here. I'm here.'

The mourners looked away, no one willing to meet his defiant gaze. Early on, before she knew anything about their liaison, Eden had asked Tara about this author, a product of the Robbin's Ferry public school system, whom Tara had recruited for the bookstore's literary series.

'Is he cute?' Eden had asked.

'I suppose so,' Tara had said carefully.

'You think I'd like him?' Eden had asked her mother playfully.

A pained expression flickered over Tara's face. 'I'm sure of it,' she had replied.

The undertaker hurried to lead Flynn and his modestly garbed companion to the front of the room. The young woman sat down and lowered her eyes. Flynn looked at the coffins in confusion, almost as if he did not know what they were doing there. He sat down heavily in a chair beside the girl in the headscarf. The undertaker introduced a Unitarian minister, who was clearly a stranger to Flynn.

The minister preached a tepid homily, and said a few generic words about mothers and sons. He made some remarks about Tara's beauty and Jeremy's feistiness that sounded as if they had been supplied by someone who hardly knew them. The undertaker leaned over Flynn and spoke into his ear. Flynn used his hand to wave away the man's concerns. He rose unsteadily to his feet and lurched toward the podium. He peered out at the assembled mourners, his gaze bleary. 'So you all show up,' he said, slurring his words.

The undertaker put a soothing hand on Flynn's sleeve, but Flynn shook him off. 'I'm doin' it,' he said irritably.

He reached into his pocket and pulled out a grimy, folded piece of paper which he flattened against the lectern.

He stared at the words for a few moments, as if mustering his forces, and then brushed at his cheeks with trembling fingers. 'Shall I compare thee,' he began, faltered, and then continued 'to a summer's day? Thou art more lovely and more temperate . . .'

He took a deep breath and read Shakespeare's love sonnet in a quavering voice. The young woman in the headscarf kept her gaze lowered, and wiped tears from her cheeks. When Flynn finished, the room was silent. He folded up his paper, jammed it in his pocket, and stumbled back to his chair.

And so, it was over. There would be no burial. Both were to be cremated after the service. The funeral director announced that there would be a brief reception at the hospitality lounge at the Cleveland Clinic, and all were invited to come.

'At the hospital? Really? Why not at their house?' Eden whispered.

'I don't think he's in any condition to host,' said Jodie disapprovingly.

'That's for sure,' said Eden.

'Besides, it's a crime scene,' said Jodie. 'Probably still blocked off by the police.'

'Do we have to go?' Eden asked.

'We have to go,' said Jodie.

As they left the funeral home, the beautiful day was fading, and storm clouds had begun to gather. Eden had cried, on and off, a good deal during the day, and felt exhausted. They found their way, with little difficulty, to the Cleveland Clinic. The hospitality lounge had all the warmth of an airport gate. They seated themselves on a molded plastic version of a loveseat in front of the plate glass windows.

Lizzy had shed her pea coat and was rushing around the lounge, putting out some functional-looking trays of sandwiches and cookies. Lizzy's husband, DeShaun, brought them each a small plastic cup of wine. Eden and Jodie both thanked him for his kindness. Eden noticed that at least half of the mourners, including her new acquaintances, Gerard and Marguerite, had foregone the chilly reception. They probably had to make dinner preparations at their café.

'Is Flynn coming?' Eden asked DeShaun.

'I think he's lying down,' said DeShaun. 'Not feeling up to it.'

'And his companion?' Jodie asked.

'Oh, I don't know. I don't really know her.'

Just then Lizzy flew by, balancing a tray of deviled eggs. DeShaun hailed her. 'Hey, honey. Who was that girl with Flynn?'

Lizzy stopped, holding the eggs aloft. 'Her name is Aaliya Saleh. She's a student at the college where he teaches. She works for him part-time as an intern.'

'What does that entail?' Jodie asked suspiciously.

DeShaun raised his eyebrows. 'With Flynn? Mostly putting out fires, I suspect.'

Lizzy gave him a reproving look. 'I understand that she's very competent. Very organized.'

'Flynn always seems to have someone to come to his rescue,' Jodie said sarcastically.

'He's suffered a terrible blow,' Lizzy reminded her.

'I don't mean to sound so critical. It's very nice of you and your husband to help out,' Jodie said.

'We're glad to help,' Lizzy said coolly. She offered the platter she was holding to Jodie. 'Egg?'

Jodie and Eden shook their heads. 'I'm not really hungry,' Eden said apologetically.

Lizzy and her husband moved on to the other guests.

'My mother would have hated this,' said Eden. 'It's so impersonal.'

'I know,' said Jodie.

'Are any of these people Flynn's family?' Eden asked.

'I don't think so. From what I understood from your mother, he just has those grandparents in Robbin's Ferry.'

'Yeah. When he called me I offered to help them get to the airport. He said they were too old and sick to make the trip. Whatever happened to his parents?'

'I guess his father was never in the picture,' said Jodie. 'The mother was a drug addict who died of an overdose in some crack house in Miami when Flynn was two. They found Flynn alone in their apartment the next day, wandering around in a filthy diaper, eating cat food that he found on the floor. His grandparents came and got him. They raised him.'

Eden grimaced. 'That's a horrible story.'

'I know,' said Jodie. 'I should have more sympathy for him. But he really acted like a lout today.'

'True enough,' Eden sighed.

They sat in silence for a moment. 'When are you headed back to the city?' Jodie asked.

'Soon. I've just been . . . paralyzed all week.'

'I'm sure you have. But you need to get back to your life.'

'I'm going to,' said Eden.

Jodie nodded and shifted in her seat. 'How's your dad doing? I always felt bad about the way my sister treated him. Hugh was so good to us. He helped put me through college. Did you know that?'

Eden shook her head.

Jodie sipped from her plastic cup. 'I always idolized your father.'

'That makes two of us,' said Eden.

'I thought my sister was so lucky to marry Hugh Radley.'

It felt a little strange to be discussing her mother's first marriage at Tara's funeral. But as a child Eden, like most children, had no real interest in the family history. Now, as an adult, she had an opportunity to satisfy her curiosity, and she was glad to take it. Besides, it wasn't as though they were besieged with people wanting to make their acquaintance. 'She said she met him at a picnic,' said Eden.

'Oh, I remember. She was still in high school but she always had boyfriends. Even then, Tara was a beauty,' Jodie reminisced. 'She came home from the picnic that night and said that she had met the guy she was going to marry.'

'Didn't your mother object? I mean, that my mom wanted to get married so young?'

'Are you kidding? My mother was ecstatic. She was a single mother herself, barely making ends meet. This was the best thing she could have hoped for. Hugh was a little bit older, he had that masonry business. He was a catch.'

'Do you think my mother really loved him?' asked Eden.

Jodie hesitated a moment. 'Your dad? Yes, she loved him,' she said firmly. 'Tara was just a little bit too young to get married. She never went to college or lived on her own. But yes, she adored Hugh.'

Eden shrugged. 'I thought so too, but what did I know? I was just a kid. They were my whole world.' Eden's voice caught in her throat. 'And then she left.'

'Well, your mother was a starry-eyed romantic and, over time, marriage becomes . . . something comfortable. If you're lucky. I think your mom just wanted some drama in her life. Another chapter. But, in the end, what did she really do but trade one man for another, one child for another?'

Eden was surprised by the bluntness of her aunt's analysis. 'That's a little harsh.'

Jodie shrugged. 'I know. I'm sorry. I guess I'm a little angry at her. She pretended everything was fine. She never even gave me a chance to . . . help her.'

Eden nodded. She understood, but didn't know how to reply. She tried to remember her mother's smiling eyes, gazing tenderly at her, but all she could think of was Tara taping shut the windows and stuffing towels under the doors. Was that why you were calling me? Eden wondered. Were you going to ask me for help? Were you giving me a chance to change your mind?

'Eden?' said Jodie. 'Have you had enough? 'Cause we can leave. We've made our appearance.'

'No one cares that we're here,' said Eden. 'Let's go.'

As they started for the door, Eden saw Lizzy out of the corner of her eye. She was hailing Eden, waving something at her. Eden stopped, and turned as Lizzy approached her.

'Are you leaving?' Lizzy asked.

Eden nodded apologetically. 'I'm exhausted,' she said.

'Headed back to New York?'

'Well, not directly. Tomorrow I'm flying home. My dad's picking me up at the local airport. I'll probably head back to New York the next day.'

'So you'll be going back to Robbin's Ferry,' said Lizzy.

'Briefly,' said Eden.

'I was just wondering if you could do us a favor.'

'Us?' said Eden.

'Flynn, really.' Lizzy was holding a program from the funeral service in her hand. 'I know that Flynn's grandparents wanted to be here but it wasn't possible for them to travel. They live in Robbin's Ferry. Flynn wanted them to have a memento from the service.'

'Couldn't he mail it to them?' Eden asked, and then cringed inwardly at how callous she sounded. Lizzy had done so much to help, and here she was, balking at one small errand.

Lizzy did not seem put off by her reaction. 'I think it would be nicer if you brought it to them. They may have questions about what happened. They're old and feeble, and it's strictly a mission of mercy, but, after all, Jeremy was their great-grandson.'

And my mother was responsible for his death, Eden added silently. 'Yes, of course,' she said, taking the program from Lizzy. 'I'll take care of it.'

'Do you need their address?' Lizzy asked.

'No. It's a small town. That's easy to find out.'

Lizzy thanked her profusely, and then excused herself to return to her hostess duties.

Jodie looked at Eden with one eyebrow raised. 'Really? They want you to make a delivery for Flynn?'

'It's all right,' said Eden with a sigh. 'It's little enough.'

Jodie shook her head. 'You're a good girl.' She tugged at Eden's sleeve. 'Now, let's get out of here, before they think of anything else.'

FOUR

Early the next morning, Eden and Jodie went to the airport and went their separate ways. Hugh picked Eden up at Westchester Airport and brought her back to the house. Eden was home in time for lunch. Gerri made sure that there were sandwiches waiting in the refrigerator. While they ate at the kitchen counter, Eden told her father about the funeral. He asked a few questions, but the pain in his eyes made Eden want to look away.

Eden brought the dishes to the sink and rinsed them. While she had her back to her father she said, 'I've actually come back with a mission.'

'What kind of mission?' Hugh asked.

'I have to take a program from the funeral service over to Flynn's grandparents. They weren't able to travel to the funeral, and one of Mom's friends asked me to bring it to them.

Hugh was silent. Eden shut the dishwasher, and turned around to look at him. He was gazing blankly out the kitchen door.

'I'm dreading it,' said Eden.

'It seems like a lot to ask of you,' said Hugh. 'Can't he just mail it to them?'

'I asked the same thing,' said Eden. 'But they're old and I'm sure they were very upset not to be able to be there. I guess it just seemed like the right thing to do. You know. Give it a personal touch.'

'I suppose,' said Hugh doubtfully.

'Would you happen to know where they live?' she asked her father.

Hugh sighed, but, in fact, there was very little about Robbin's Ferry which he did not know. He knew the Darbys' street, and described the house.

'Okay. Well, I think I'll just go and get it over with,' said Eden. 'I won't be staying long.'

Following her father's directions, Eden drove to one of the older neighborhoods in Robbin's Ferry, on a tree-lined street that ended at the river. The Darby house was, as Hugh had described it, the eyesore of the neighborhood. It was a split-level, probably built in the 1950s, and its gray asbestos shingles were covered with grime. It was surrounded by newer, or more recently renovated houses, but the Darby house sat on its immensely valuable lot, stubbornly unimproved, with a wheelchair ramp which did nothing to enhance the house's façade. There was a fanlike arrangement of small American flags in a metal holder atop the railing on the ramp. A US Marine decal, reading *Semper Fi*, obscured the small window at the top of the front door. The linings of the drawn curtains in the house's other windows were unevenly stained with yellow, like old teeth. On the top floor of the house there was a window with cardboard standing in for a missing pane. The yard was large and seemed mostly untended. Even now, in winter, Eden could see that the bushes and trees around it were straggly.

Eden steeled herself, and got out of the car. She walked up to the front door. There was a metal knocker, but it hung askew. Eden knocked on the door.

There were sounds of life coming from behind the door. Finally it was answered, the door dragged across a matted shag rug of faded, indeterminate color. The man who opened the door was old and wiry, and colorless as the house itself.

He wore his white hair in a short crew cut, and his face was etched with lines. The afternoon sun reflected off his steel-rimmed glasses.

'Yes?' he demanded.

'Mr Darby? My name is Eden Radley. I . . . my mother was married to your grandson . . . that is . . .'

'I know who you are,' he said abruptly.

Eden nodded. 'I just got back from Cleveland, from the funeral. Your grandson asked me to bring you something.'

'Come in,' barked the scrawny old man, turning his back on her. He shuffled away from the door, slightly stooped, but with no other obvious physical impairment. Eden followed him into the living room. The furniture was worn, and the room was hot and stuffy. A skinny old woman wearing a pink sweat-suit sat slumped in a wheelchair, an afghan over her knees. Her thin white hair was fluffy around her face.

Flynn's grandfather flopped down into a Barcalounger beside his wife. 'Company, old girl,' he said. He did not offer Eden a seat.

The old woman peered up at Eden, as if she had difficulty with her vision. 'Who is it, Michael?' she asked in a querulous voice.

Eden walked over to the wheelchair and bent over, offering the old woman her hand. 'I'm Eden Radley. My mother was married to Flynn. Your grandson. I've just come back from the funeral.'

'Whose funeral?' the woman asked in confusion.

'Her mother's,' Michael Darby shouted at his wife. 'And Flynn's kid. I told you about this. The mother killed herself. Took the boy with her.'

The old woman pressed her lips together and tears rose to her rheumy eyes.

'Oh yes. Terrible. Just terrible.' She clutched Eden's warm hand in a cold, clawlike grip.

Eden disengaged and straightened up. 'I understood that you couldn't make it because of your health.'

'We could have made it. He didn't want us there,' said Michael.

Looking at the two of them, Eden doubted very much if

they could have negotiated hotels and airports. Not without considerable help. And, judging from the deteriorating condition of the house, help was in short supply for these two.

'Well, in any case,' she said, 'I brought you both a copy of the program from the funeral service. Flynn wanted you to have it.'

'Oh he did, did he?' said the old man combatively. 'That would be the first time he ever thought of us.'

'Michael, don't be like that,' said the old woman in her thin, plaintive voice. She looked up at Eden hopefully. 'Flynn is a nice boy. He always tried his best. He had a lot of problems.'

'Nice boy, my ass. He was always nothing but trouble,' said Michael Darby.

For a moment, Eden almost felt sorry for Flynn. 'Well, he wanted you to have this.' She put the program in the old woman's hands.

The paper shook as Flynn's grandmother held it, frowning at the picture. 'Who are they?' she asked.

Michael Darby's pale cheeks reddened. 'I told you,' he cried. 'Flynn's wife and kid.'

The old woman's eyes softened. 'She's very pretty,' she said. She looked up at Eden. 'She looks like you!'

Eden did not know what to say. 'Thank you,' she said.

'How is Flynn?' asked the old woman.

Eden shrugged. 'He's . . . having a hard time.'

'Why a hard time?' Flynn's grandfather demanded.

'His wife and child are dead,' said Eden, affronted by his tone.

'Are you kidding me?' said Michael Darby. 'His wife was old enough to be his mother, and the kid was nothing but a drooling mess. It's a blessing he got rid of both of them. Your mother did him a favor, checking out like that. Flynn's on easy street now. Got the life insurance for the both of them. He'll be off on a world cruise. No, we won't see him again. He won't come back here until we die and he can get his hands on this house and make a bundle selling it to some developer who will pay him a king's ransom to knock it down. You mark my words. All we sacrificed for him, and for what?'

Somewhere in the middle of this diatribe, Eden realized that this visit to the grandparents must not have been Flynn's idea at all. This was just something that Lizzy, in her innocence, thought would be nice. A nice idea in theory, Eden thought. But, in reality, completely pointless. 'Well,' she said brusquely, 'I've delivered the program to you. I'm going to go now.'

'Oh, don't go,' the old woman pleaded. 'Stay and have some cookies. Do we have cookies, Michael?'

'I don't know,' Michael grumbled, twisting forward to get out of his chair. 'I'll check.'

'Don't bother,' said Eden. 'I can't stay. I'll show myself out.'

'Please stay. Make her stay, Michael,' cried Flynn's grand-mother.

'Leave her alone, Mother,' Michael said in a long-suffering tone. 'She wants to go. Let her go.'

Eden did not hesitate. She left the house without a backward look. She was shaking as she drove home. The old man was so vile, that it made her wonder what Flynn's years growing up had been like. Obviously, raising Flynn after his mother died was not something they had undertaken willingly. How often did his grandfather remind him of that? she wondered. How could Flynn ever have felt at home in that house?

When she got home, exhausted by the whole ordeal, Eden went up to her room and took a nap. She was awakened by her father gently shaking her. The afternoon dusk was deep-ening into night.

'Sweetie, don't you think you ought to go back?' he asked.

'You want me to leave?' Eden asked plaintively.

'No,' said Hugh. 'But I know you should. You have work.'

Eden knew he was right. It was time. Even though she was eager to escape the memories which surrounded her here, she dreaded saying goodbye to her father, who looked utterly drained after the week's events. It was only his urging that forced her out of the nest.

At the train station, she kissed him tenderly on the cheek and noticed how pale and papery his skin seemed. They embraced for a long time.

'I'm worried about you, Dad. You seem . . . a little tired,' Eden said, sniffling into a tissue.

'I'm fine,' Hugh said. 'Don't worry about me. Stop worrying.'

Eden hugged him again, thanked him for everything and

climbed aboard the train. She found a seat and leaned her forehead against the cold train window. Although it was only a short, thirty-five-minute ride on the train from Robbin's Ferry to New York City, the psychological distance was vast. By the time Eden had reached Grand Central, and taken the subway out to Brooklyn, the winter day had grown dark. The subway was a short walk from her apartment, which was on the second floor of a brownstone, in the front. A bay window, nearly obscured by the branches of a London plane tree, looked out over the city street. A fabric artist who lived in the next block had come in to water her plants, and left the lights on, as Eden had requested. She couldn't bear to come home to complete darkness. There was enough of that in her life at the moment. Eden let herself in. Her friend had left a note of condolence and a little box of candy on the table. Eden felt both relieved and lonesome to be back in her own place, her own world.

She was looking glumly into her empty refrigerator when she got a call.

Her friend Jasmine, who was a waitress at the Black Cat across the street, was purring in her ear. 'You're back?' Jasmine said. 'Come over here. Right now. Have dinner with your friends.'

Eden hesitated, but only for a moment. 'Ten minutes,' she said.

FIVE

The dinner was a little awkward at first, but a few drinks, and universal good intentions, smoothed out the evening. Eden's friends would not allow her to pay for anything. She looked around fondly at the motley group of actors and bloggers, artists and waiters who had gathered to welcome her back, with no questions asked. The topic of her loss was avoided by tacit agreement. It was not a subject to be discussed in a large, lively group. But their banter distracted her, and their concern for her was palpable. She felt lucky to be among them. Late in the evening, Vince, the bartender from the Brisbane Tavern, came in and was immediately invited to join their table. Eden could feel his gaze on her during the evening and they exchanged a nod and a smile. He was undeniably attractive, and ordinarily she might have flirted with him, but she was too exhausted tonight, and too fragile. She sank into the supportive kindness of those at the cheerful table like a warm bath, and when she got up to leave, she quickly accepted the offer from her gay barista friend, Drew, to walk her back to her apartment.

She barely slept, and thought about calling in sick when the alarm went off, but, finally, Eden told herself that she would have to face it sooner or later, and there was no point in putting off the inevitable. She wore sunglasses on the subway to Manhattan, even though the day was cloudy, and, when she entered the building on 57th Street, she avoided eye contact with anyone she passed. In the elevator she kept her gaze straight ahead. Even though she recognized some of the people who worked at DeLaurier Publishing, she pretended not to see them. She entered the reception area and waved at Melissa without stopping to chat.

Once she was burrowed in her own office, she felt safer, and the anxious racing of her heart settled down to a normal rhythm. A bouquet of flowers arrived from the company, and were set on her desk. Sophy came in, as she always did, and settled herself in the chair in front of Eden, ready to listen. Sophy could be a wonderfully matter-of-fact person, and she did not avoid the difficult subject of the murder/suicide. Her questions were both unabashed and tactful. Eden admitted helplessly that she could not explain it, and Sophy agreed that it was utterly baffling. Somehow, Eden felt better. She had said it out loud to someone who did not know her family, and she had not turned to stone as a result. It would be easier to say it aloud the next time.

Work had piled up on her desk and computer, and even though she had little appetite for it, she forced herself to begin working on manuscripts. Gradually, she found her interest returning. She hid out in her office for the rest of the work

day, and no one tried to coax her out. When her mind wandered from the task, she chided herself into refocusing. She was lucky to have a job that interested her. Getting back to work felt like a relief.

Over the next few days, life as it was, far from Robbin's Ferry, began to resume a semblance of normalcy. Eden called her father every night, reassured by the sound of Hugh's voice. Her friends were solicitous, and invited her to dinner. She ate in someone else's kitchen, or as their guest in one bistro or another, for the better part of two weeks. Her crying jags became less frequent. Her mother's suicide had been a shock and a loss, but, in many ways, she told herself, she had grieved for her mother years ago. When Tara left Hugh for Flynn Darby, life as Eden knew it was torn apart. While Tara's death was much more final, the feeling of losing her mother was not new to her. She had survived it once, she reminded herself. She would survive again.

One day Hugh called, and asked if he could come into Manhattan and take her out to dinner after work. Eden was surprised, but glad for the opportunity to see him. After they had eaten at a Chinese restaurant on the West Side, Hugh got around to the purpose of his visit. 'I'm going to Florida for two weeks,' he said.

Eden was delighted to hear that news. 'Oh Dad, that's great. You gonna do some fishing?'

'I hope so,' he said. 'I've been a little worried about going so far away from you at such a difficult time.'

'I'll be fine,' Eden reassured him. 'My friends are looking after me. I haven't had dinner alone since I got back.'

'Are you sure you're okay?' he asked.

'I'm okay,' said Eden, and she did not allow even a shade of sadness into her voice. She wanted him to go to Florida, and rest in the sun, without worrying about her. 'Who are you going with?' she asked. 'Are you going by yourself?'

Hugh looked a little pained. 'Actually. No. Um . . . I'm going with Gerri. Her cousin has a condo down there that he's lending us for the week.'

'Gerri?' said Eden, taken aback. 'I thought you two were just . . . friends.'

'We are friends,' Hugh said firmly. 'And my friend asked me if I wanted to go to Florida.'

'Okay,' said Eden slowly. 'How long have you known about this?'

'Not long. It was kind of spur of the moment.'

'Dad, you're not spontaneous,' said Eden.

Hugh smiled shyly. 'Okay, okay. It's something we talked about on and off for a while. Gerri was thinking of asking her cousin, and then the cousin just called and offered. So, it seemed like . . . the thing to do.'

'Well, great,' said Eden, trying to mean it. My father is going away with a girlfriend, and I can't even get a date, she thought. But whatever.

'I'll miss you,' he said sincerely.

'It's only two weeks,' said Eden.

'I always miss you,' he said.

'I know, Dad. Listen. You have a wonderful time.'

Their parting was fond, but not sad. Eden was proud of herself for that. Part of her wanted to just climb into his pocket and stay there. But her life had to go on.

And so did his.

A few days after she bid her father farewell, Eden got a call from Rob Newsome, the editorial director.

'Eden,' he said. 'Mr DeLaurier would like us to come to a meeting in his office at four o'clock.'

'What's it about?' she asked. She had never been summoned by the publisher before. It was a family business, one of the few left in New York publishing, which had been started by Maurice DeLaurier's great-uncle nearly a hundred years earlier. Maurice was widely considered to be a shrewd CEO, who had grown the business from the small house it had been when he inherited it. Eden had met him when Rob Newsome hired her, but after that she had done little more than exchange polite greetings with the impeccably turned-out executive.

'A new project. I really can't say any more than that. I'll see you at Maurice's office at four.'

'Okay,' said Eden.

At four o'clock she refreshed her make-up, straightened her form-fitting knit dress, and walked down the corridor toward the publisher's office. She got a nod to enter from his assistant. Eden tapped on the door then went in. The office had a wall of windows overlooking 57th Street, and the afternoon sun had turned the room, which was lined with bookshelves and furnished in leather and rich-looking carpets, to a blinding red gold. Eden closed the door and approached the conversation area where the two men were sitting. Maurice DeLaurier stood up politely and indicated a club chair.

'Eden, thanks for coming. Won't you have a seat?'

She glanced at Rob, and sat down in the empty chair.

'It's good to see you back at work. You've been through a difficult time.'

'Thank you for the flowers,' said Eden. Although she doubted that he even knew about the flowers, he nodded graciously.

'Little enough,' he said, 'under the circumstances. Now, if you don't mind, I'll come straight to the point. I've asked you both here because I've been having some conversations with Gideon Lendl. He has made us a most interesting proposal.'

Eden immediately recognized the name of one of the most powerful literary agents in New York. 'Gideon Lendl himself?' she asked. She knew that it was unusual for Gideon Lendl to personally represent an author. His authors tended to be quite literary but also commercial, often landing on the best-seller list. Usually, the bigger, better-known publishing houses landed Gideon Lendl's clients. She felt a little thrill of excitement at this news.

She glanced at Rob. His face was expressionless and his eyes were fixed on the publisher. Eden felt as if he was avoiding her questioning gaze. She turned back to Maurice. 'Is it a celebrity author?' she asked. They were all well aware of the clout a celebrity could bring to the sales of a book.

Maurice shook his head. 'No. Up to this point, this author has only published in small literary magazines. But circumstances conspire to make this a very interesting property. I must tell you that the situation is a little delicate, though.'

Any book which was being fronted by Gideon Lendl himself was bound to be an important property. What does this have to do with me? she wondered. She had worked closely on big books with various editors in the company, but had not handled any major projects herself.

As if he had read her mind, Maurice addressed her. 'Eden, this particular book has . . . personal implications for you.'

'For me?' she queried.

Maurice pressed his lips together and leaned forward. 'Eden, the author wants you to be the editor of this book.'

'Me? Why in the world? Do I know the author?'

Maurice nodded. 'In fact, you do. His name is Flynn Darby. I believe he was married to your late mother.'

If Maurice DeLaurier had smacked her across the face, he could not have stunned her more effectively. Eden blinked at him, as if trying to summon her senses after a knockout punch.

'Mr Darby is a very talented writer, and the novel he has written makes for compelling reading. But, I feel I must warn you that it's . . . somewhat grim, and very clearly about his life with your mother. There's a great deal in there about their . . . marriage, and their struggles with a disabled child. Apparently, Mr Darby had been working on it for several years, and it was nearly finished when this terrible tragedy occurred.'

Eden stared at Maurice DeLaurier. The publisher was about to offer her a chance to instantly gain status in the company. In the publishing world in general. All she had to do was betray her family. She felt the old familiar hatred for Flynn Darby wash over her, and she began to shake all over. 'And now, my mother's suicide, my half-brother's . . .' She couldn't bring herself to say 'murder'. 'It would be good for sales,' she said bluntly.

'Eden,' Rob said in a warning voice.

'Sorry,' she mumbled.

'Eden,' Maurice said kindly, 'I'm the one who's sorry. I realize how difficult this must be for you. I don't have to tell you that authors cannibalize their lives rather shamelessly. Frankly, it can be a little . . . repulsive from time to time. Your stepfather is far from the only writer who has chosen to do this. No sooner does a personal tragedy occur than many an author is trying to use it to advance his or her career. Mr Darby is not unusual in that regard.'

Eden was not able to look him in the eye.

'But I have to be very honest with you,' said Maurice. 'The timing on this, while unfortunate in some ways, is very significant for us. It makes his book very topical. This book has the potential to be a major best-seller. First of all, it's very well written. I want you to know that. This isn't some hack job. Then, there is the disability angle, which he handles sympathetically. And then, undeniably your mother's tragic death and the death of their son—'

'Gives it currency,' said Eden in a dull voice.

'It's an important opportunity,' said Maurice.

She shuddered and turned to Rob. 'Did you know about this?' she asked him.

'Maurice emailed me the book last night,' Rob said evenly. 'He wanted me to know what we were wading into here. Obviously, if you choose to do it, I would be advising you. It's a lot to take on.'

'And me being the editor would also be a talking point, I suppose,' she said, trying to sound matter-of-fact.

'Eden, this is a business,' said Rob. 'Of course it would beneficial for publicity purposes to have you as an editor.'

'I'm sure that's why Flynn asked for me,' she said.

'Well, I asked Gideon about this,' said Maurice. 'He feels that Mr Darby sincerely wants your input on this. You know more about the people involved than any other editor could possibly know. Mr Darby acknowledged to Gideon that you might not be willing to work with him.'

'He realized that, did he?' she asked.

'He did, but he asked Gideon to put this forward to you anyway.'

Eden took a deep breath and stared at a spot on Maurice's desk. How could she possibly do this? How could she work closely with Flynn Darby, knowing that he was using her mother's death as a way to promote his career? How could she ever explain it to her father? He would be appalled. 'And if I don't agree to do it?' she asked. 'Will I lose my job?'

'Oh heavens, no,' Maurice demurred. 'Don't even think such a thing.'

Eden studied the publisher's face and body language. He was being sincere to a point, she thought. He would not fire her for refusing. But she would not soon be forgiven for her refusal to cooperate.

'It should be said,' Rob interjected, 'that if you don't take this project on, it may not stay with our company. Flynn Darby could have his pick of publishers.'

Maurice shook his head. The paterfamilias. 'Rob, don't do that. Don't try to pressure her that way.'

Eden felt as if she would explode with frustration. It seemed like a cruel double blow that Flynn had put her in this position of jeopardizing her own career if she said no to his book. 'I understand the consequences,' she said.

'Look, Eden,' said Maurice. 'We may be getting ahead of ourselves here. Why don't you read the book first before you make a decision? I think you may be surprised by it. It's really quite good. Of course, you would be looking at it from a very different perspective. But give it a read, and try to keep an open mind while you're reading. If you decide that you cannot do it, I will respect your choice.'

There was no way out of this trap, and Eden knew it. She had to at least look at the book, and respond. Or be seen as completely intransigent and unreasonable.

Once again, Flynn had given her no choice. 'All right,' she said. 'I'll read it.'

Rob stood up. Maurice followed suit.

'We'll need an answer very soon,' said Maurice.

'You'll have one,' said Eden. She got up and smoothed down her dress. 'I'll read it tonight.'

SIX

By the time she got home from work, Eden's head was pounding. So this is what a migraine is like, she thought. The thudding in her head made her feel sick to her stomach. Every step was jarring, every smell sickening. She was supposed to have dinner with her friend, Shelley, a masseuse who lived and worked in a converted factory in Red

Hook. She texted Shelley a message that she could not make it tonight. She pulled the shades, took about four aspirin and lay down on her bed, with all the lights turned off in the apartment, and a washrag on her forehead.

Sleep, she thought. I have to sleep. Anything to escape.

But she couldn't sleep. All she could do was think about Flynn Darby, who was now going to profit handsomely from Tara's suicide, from Jeremy's pitiful death. And what role would Eden play in this profit-taking? If she agreed to do it, she would feel like a traitor to her father, to herself, to her mother's memory. If she refused, Flynn would have another editor in no time, and she would be denied even the possibility of some influence on this very public version of her mother's life. He was a user, and he had put her into an impossible position. There was no way that she was going to be in the right.

She went over and over the same territory in her mind, and then, somehow, she was blessedly released from consciousness. She fell into a deep sleep, and was awakened by the ringing of her phone. She blinked and looked around. The ringing was coming from her bag on the floor beside her bed. The bag which contained her iPad. The iPad which contained Flynn Darby's book. She rummaged angrily in the bag, pulled out the phone and snapped into the receiver. 'Yes?'

'Eden, it's Vince. From the Brisbane.'

She was not expecting to hear from him, and wasn't sure that she wanted to. It was difficult to get enthused at the idea of getting to know someone right now. But even if it had been someone she longed to hear from, she wouldn't have been able to respond. 'Hi, Vince. Look, I can't talk,' she mumbled. 'I have a horrible headache.' As soon as she said it, however, she noted that the headache was much better after that deep sleep. Still, the only thing she wanted was more sleep.

'Oh, sorry to hear that,' he said.

'Yeah, I'm sorry too. It's been a tough day. Another time,' she said, ending the call. No sooner had she slipped the phone back into her bag and turned over on the bed than she was asleep again.

*   *   *

Someone pounding a nail into the wall in her dream became impossible to ignore. As soon as she began to question it in the dream, she commenced the swim to the surface of consciousness. The damp rag, which had been on her forehead, was now lodged, cold and wet, under her neck, and she could see that darkness had fallen outside. The sound of pounding in her dream was, she now realized, coming from the door of her apartment.

Eden forced herself to sit up and then stand. She touched her head gingerly, but the headache had abated, and she felt a surge of gratitude for the end of that misery. If only that hammering on her door didn't make it start up again.

'Coming,' she shouted. She shuffled to the front door in her stocking feet, a hoody pulled on over her knit dress. She glanced in the mirror by the door and saw that her make-up was smudged under her bleary eyes, and her hair looked as if someone had combed it with an egg beater.

Eden sighed and opened the door without taking off the chain. She looked quizzically at the man in the hallway through the narrow opening.

Vince, the bartender, was standing there, holding a fragrant brown paper bag adorned with the Black Cat logo. 'Hi, Eden,' he said.

'How did you get in the building?' she demanded irritably.

'Someone was going out and held the door for me,' he admitted.

'How did you even find out where I lived?'

Vince shrugged. 'I asked your friend Jasmine. I told her you had a migraine and I wanted to bring you some of those Thai spring rolls from the Black Cat. Food can really help when you have a headache like that.'

'And just like that, she told you where I lived?' Eden demanded.

'Well, I asked her for your address.'

Just then, the elevator door opened behind him, and Jasmine emerged, carrying a six-pack of Coke. Jasmine waved at the opening in the door.

'Hi, Eden,' she said. 'How are you feeling, sweetie? Vince came in the restaurant and told me you had a migraine, so we got you this takeout and I stopped at the corner and bought you some Coke. That's always good for a headache. Can we come in?'

Eden realized, a bit sheepishly, that there was no harm intended here. Vince was not trying to muscle his way into her place. He just decided to do something nice. The two of them were in collusion. They were being solicitous. Shamed by her own assumptions, she unlatched the chain and opened the door.

'Come on in,' she said. 'I'm a mess. Don't even look at me.'

'You look fine,' said Vince.

'Please, don't be gallant,' Eden said. 'Put the stuff on the table.'

Vince set the bag on the table, and Jasmine went and put the six-pack of Coke in the refrigerator, pulling out a couple and offering one each to Eden and to Vince. Eden took hers gratefully. Vince hesitated.

'Well, sit,' said Eden. She looked into the bag and began to unpack round aluminum containers with plastic lids. 'Wow, you brought a feast here.'

'We weren't sure what would appeal to you besides the spring rolls,' Vince said.

Eden was beginning to feel ashamed of her ill humor. 'Have you two eaten?'

Vince shrugged. 'I'm not that hungry,' he said.

'Well, I'm starved,' said Jasmine. 'You two sit down at the table. I'll get the plates.'

All awkwardness fled as the three of them tucked into the take-out. They chatted companionably, and Vince flirted amiably with them both. Why not? Eden thought. She was just glad to be here with them on this most trying of days. She felt as if she had never eaten a meal that tasted so good. Vince, who had professed not to be hungry, was licking his fingers in satisfaction.

'Thank you,' said Eden. 'Really. I can't thank you enough. Both of you. I really felt wretched when I got home from work. I can't remember ever feeling that bad from a headache.'

'What brought it on?' Vince asked.

Jasmine shot him a warning glance. 'She's under a lot of stress.'

Vince, belatedly, looked uneasy. 'Of course,' he said. 'Your mother's death.'

Eden sighed, and pushed back from the table. 'No, though, it was something related to it that brought it on.' She hesitated. She knew they wouldn't press her if she decided not to explain it. But she found that she wanted to tell them. She wanted to bounce it off people who weren't involved.

'My publisher called me in today,' she said. 'It seems that the house has been offered an important first novel, and the author wants me to edit it.'

'That's good, right?' said Jasmine, starting to stash the clutter of containers and napkins into the Black Cat bag.

'The author is my stepfather, and the book is based on his marriage to my mother, and about their lives with my now late half-brother, who suffered from a rare genetic disorder.'

Vince's eyes widened over the napkin he had pressed to his lips. He lowered the napkin and frowned at her. 'Okay, don't be mad at me for asking, but doesn't it seem like he is trying to capitalize on recent events?'

'Yes,' said Eden. 'Exactly. My mother killed herself and her son by carbon monoxide poisoning. My publisher insists that the book has great literary merit. But obviously, this murder/suicide gives the book built-in publicity. They gave me until tomorrow to decide if I want to go along with this.'

'That's disgusting,' Jasmine exclaimed. 'How could he even think of exploiting their deaths this way?'

'I know,' Eden agreed.

'Still . . .' said Vince.

'Still what?' Eden asked.

'I know this is going to sound cold, but, let's be realistic. Of all the books published every month, how many have this kind of . . . story attached to them? It's a public relations coup.'

'That doesn't make it right,' said Jasmine indignantly.

'I'm not saying it does. Just stating facts,' said Vince. 'Look at it this way, Eden. Someone's going to publish this book. Why should your stepfather be the only one to profit from this tragedy? If it can help your career, why shouldn't you do it?'

'Ever the businessman,' said Jasmine. 'That's why you own the Brisbane and I'm still a waitress.'

'You own the Brisbane?' Eden asked, surprised.

Vince shrugged and smiled. 'Yup. You figured I was an actor, right?'

'Or a would-be writer,' Eden admitted wryly.

Vince shook his head. 'Nope. I work there, and I live above the store. Not exactly glamorous but it's mine.'

'That's quite a coup in this neighborhood,' Eden observed.

'I worked briefly on Wall Street, years ago. I was good at it but I hated it. So I took my ill-gotten gains and bought the building. That's why I've got all this gray hair. But never mind that. We were talking about you.'

Eden had to admit to herself that she looked at him with a new respect. He understood the problem. And he saw the big picture dispassionately. Something she was not able to do.

'What are you going to do?' Jasmine asked.

Eden frowned and was silent for a minute. 'I don't know. I'm sure you're right, Vince, but it makes me sick just to think of it. I guess the first thing I'm going to do is read the book, so I can support my position coherently.'

All three nodded thoughtfully. Then Vince stood up. 'Well, we better get out of here, Jasmine. Reading a whole book is gonna take a while. So you have to read it tonight?' he asked, looking at Eden.

She nodded. 'I have to force myself to.'

'Well, don't get another headache,' said Jasmine, ruffling Eden's hair as she passed by her on the way to the kitchen. 'I'm putting these leftovers in your fridge.'

Eden thanked them again. After they put on their coats and collected their belongings, she walked the two of them to the door. She watched, almost enviously, as they went out into the hallway, teasing one another playfully.

Jasmine punched Vince in his upper arm.

Could be something developing there, Eden thought, watching them. Part of her felt happy at that idea, and part of her felt jealous. No, she insisted to herself. If that's what happens, it's a good thing. All I know is, I just wish I were going with them. Away from here. Anywhere. Anything but the task which was facing her. The book she was going to have to read. But there was no point in resisting. Just start it, she told herself. You don't have to read the whole thing to be able to say no. Just enough to make a case for why you can't do it.

She shuffled into her bedroom, took off her clothes and put on a warm bathrobe. Then she slid into her bed. She turned on the light attached to the headboard, picked up her iPad and began to read.

SEVEN

Eden tapped on the open door to Rob's office.

'Come in,' he said. His graying, close-cropped head was bent over his PC. His shirtsleeves were rolled up, his jacket hung across the back of his chair.

Eden stuck her head in. 'Your assistant isn't at her desk.'

'Eden!' he exclaimed. 'Sit down. Let me finish this email and I'll be right with you.'

She went in and sat in front of the editorial director's desk. She glanced at the framed photos of Rob's smiling family on his desktop, and then she glanced at her own reflection in his office window. She had been up all night, and there were dark circles under her eyes, and folds of exhaustion in her face. She had taken a shower and washed and blown out her hair first thing this morning after she finished the book. She had put on a charcoal-gray military-style jacket that felt like a suit of armor to her. It usually made her feel sharp and in control. However, sharp and in control were the last things she was feeling this morning.

'There,' said Rob. 'Send. Now, how are you doing? I assume you're here about Flynn Darby's book.'

'I am,' she said.

'You had a chance to read it?'

Eden nodded. 'I read all night.'

'And? What did you think?'

Eden gave the book her most valuable compliment. 'I couldn't put it down.'

Rob nodded, deliberately keeping his response noncommittal. 'That was how I felt when I read it,' he said.

Despite her positive reaction, Eden was unsmiling. She had wanted to hate it. She was prepared to hate it. Even now, she was telling herself that the only reason she found it fascinating was the opportunity it afforded to have a look inside her mother's second marriage. That had been irresistible to her.

Rob waited for her to elaborate. Finally he said, 'It's a very powerful book.'

'Rob, I can't help feeling resentful that he now wants to use the death of his family – of my mother and my half-brother – for promotional purposes,' she said angrily.

Rob tented his fingers and pressed them to his lips before he spoke. 'I can understand you feeling that way, of course,' he said. 'But he couldn't have known that this would happen when he was writing it.'

Eden sighed. 'No, I suppose not. He doesn't even address it in the book.'

'Well, it has to be addressed. The book may need to open with that, and then go back to the beginning,' Rob mused. 'Or maybe just a very matter-of-fact recounting at the end. It's not clear which way to go.' He peered at her. 'So, I guess, this is the big question – do you want to take a whack at it, or would you rather pass?'

'I'd rather pass,' said Eden. 'It's sickening, it's so close.'

Rob nodded, avoiding her gaze.

'But if I pass, it will just be sent somewhere else, and someone who doesn't give a damn will take it on. I don't want that. I'd rather be the one who sees it through. Gets it into print.'

Rob kept his enthusiasm tempered. 'Don't agree to this if it feels wrong to you. You don't have to do it, you know. There will be other books.'

'I know,' said Eden. Although she knew what he was not saying. There would never be another book of this significance aimed directly at her. There would never be another such opportunity. In her mind's eye, she was seeing a flashing review of those pages she had read. How this thinly disguised couple met, and both realized that they were at a crossroads

in their lives. According to Flynn's account, they struggled
not to succumb to their emotions. The daunting age difference
between them and the female character's reluctance to leave
her long marriage and her daughter made the situation seem
bleak. Hopeless. And yet, they knew that they had to be
together. With the birth of their son, they felt new hope. And
then, their hopes were dashed. They uprooted their lives and
moved to be near the doctor who offered them the best hope
for their child's terrible, mystifying condition. The woman
secretly blamed herself, wondering if perhaps her child's illness
was some sort of cosmic retribution for the pain she had caused
her first husband, her daughter.

Eden had wondered, when she read that part, how Flynn
had known it. Was it just something he suspected? Or were he
and her mother so open with one another that Tara had been
able to tell him her most secret fears, her worst suspicions?
Somehow, Eden suspected the latter. Either way, it gave Eden
a guilty, but undeniable, feeling of satisfaction to think that
Tara had blamed herself, had suffered because of how she had
treated Hugh and Eden. And, she felt a grudging admiration
for Flynn, who could have left that out, and never mentioned
it. It was fiction, after all. But it was fiction based on truth,
and the truth which supported it gave the book its gravity, its
sense of reality.

The entire book had a feeling of impending doom which
kept Eden caught up in it the whole way. She even found
herself hoping that it would all work out for them. Knowing
that it did not. 'I want to do it. I want this book to be mine,'
she said.

'That is great news,' said Rob. 'Let me call Maurice.'

'Yes,' she said, with a certainty undermined by anxiety. 'Tell
him I'm in.'

Negotiations for the purchase of the book began within a few
days, and Eden was kept abreast of the process, although Rob
and Maurice were at the forefront of the financial discussions.
Eden never heard from Flynn in the course of the negotiations.
Gideon Lendl represented Flynn's interests ably. When the
purchase price was finally decided, Eden was forced to question

anew her participation in this project. Flynn was going to be handsomely compensated to tell the story of his marriage, now immensely more interesting because of the murder/suicide of his wife and son.

The news of his success was to be conveyed to him by his literary agent. Gideon Lendl assured Eden that Flynn would be informed immediately.

The thought of it made Eden feel queasy. Rob invited her to Maurice's office to celebrate with a glass of champagne. Eden went, knowing that she had to share in this celebration.

Maurice lifted his glass. 'To great reviews, and great sales,' he said. 'And to Eden, for taking on this difficult project.'

'I'll do my best to do a good job on it.'

'I know you will,' said Rob.

For the next two days, she expected to hear from Flynn, thanking her, perhaps, for taking on his book. But he remained silent. Was it her place to call him? And say what? Congratulations on cannibalizing my family history for personal gain? Stop, she told herself. You agreed to this. You can no longer blame this entirely on him. Still, she could not help but feel that her acquiescence was a favor to him, and that he owed her his gratitude. She felt trapped in a standoff, and she didn't know exactly how to proceed. She felt stupid having to ask for guidance, first thing out of the gate. But she finally decided that she was in need of a little advice.

She went down to Rob's office and knocked on the door. He asked her to come in and offered her a seat. 'What's up?' he said. 'No second thoughts, I hope.'

'No. It's just . . . I'm not sure about the protocol here,' Eden said. 'Do I call Flynn and ask for a meeting, or what?'

'Yes. I was thinking about this. It probably would be a good idea for you to arrange to go out there to Ohio to meet with him. That way you can confer directly over the manuscript. There's still a great deal of work to be done and it might be best to begin the process face to face. DeLaurier will pick up your expenses for the time there.'

'Isn't this normally done electronically? I mean, that's been my experience.'

'Well, normally, yes. But this is kind of a . . . delicate situation,' said Rob. 'You two have a personal history, and you are dealing with the aftermath of a tragedy. A lot depends on the relationship you have going forward. There's going to be some publicity which might prove awkward for the two of you. No use in pretending otherwise. The more closely you work together on this, the better. We want you to have a united front when it comes to the handling and promotion of this book. How do you and your stepfather normally get along?'

'I've hardly ever spoken to him,' said Eden.

Rob looked startled. 'Really?'

Eden shrugged. 'There was a lot of bad feeling. That part of the book was painfully accurate.'

'I'm sorry. I didn't realize . . .'

'That's why I was so shocked that he wanted me to be his editor.'

Rob nodded. 'Well, in that case, I definitely think it would be best for you two to begin the work in person. Do you have a problem with that?'

'No,' said Eden, but her stomach felt queasy. 'I just wasn't sure . . .'

'The situation is a bit unusual,' Rob agreed. 'But I think you should go out there and try to . . . come to a meeting of minds.'

The memory of her recent trip to Cleveland, for her mother's funeral, weighed heavily on Eden. The prospect of repeating that trip filled her with dread. Be a professional, she chided herself. No one forced you to do this. 'All right,' she said, standing up. 'I'll get the ball rolling.'

EIGHT

The arrangements were businesslike, and done by email between Eden and Flynn. Eden called her father in Florida to tell him that she was going out to Cleveland to see an author she had met at her mother's funeral – one of Tara's friends – who had subsequently brought his book to

DeLaurier. Her father sounded happily preoccupied and didn't question it, other than to remark that it was ironic that she was going there again, after spending a lifetime without ever setting foot in Ohio. He was proud of the way she was sometimes required to travel for business. To Hugh, it seemed a sign of her success, that her company would pay for her to fly out to meet authors. It wasn't the first time she had been on such a mission. She couldn't bear to tell him the truth of who she was going to meet.

She flew out to Cleveland from Kennedy, and picked up her rental car. She had reserved a one-bedroom unit at the Garden Suites hotel not far from the airport. When she arrived, Eden was pleased to see that the room, though unprepossessing, was, as advertised, more like an apartment than a hotel room. It had a living room and a dining area, as well as a small bedroom. The sliding glass doors, all unbreakable and safely locked, faced out onto a small courtyard which was bleak in the winter chill, with a few scrawny trees, and snow piled against the building and beneath a pair of garden benches. All the furnishings in the apartment-sized room were well worn and nondescript. Still, a layout of this size would have cost a thousand dollars a night in New York City, she thought. Here, the price was rock bottom and reasonable. Eden pulled the stiffly lined drapes closed, unpacked quickly and set up her electronics. She lay down on the plaid double bedspread and tried to take a nap, but it was no use. Her nerves were on edge.

Finally, she got up and went down to the desk to ask where she might buy a few basic supplies. The pudgy young man in his maroon Garden Suites V-neck pullover directed her to a convenience store down the block. Eden elected to walk, and was amazed at how the damp cold cut through her. The road to the convenience store was quiet, almost dead, except for the roar of planes arriving and departing overhead. The store was haphazardly stocked, but she carried back some water bottles and a few things for breakfast. She had noticed that the room had a coffee maker, and she liked the idea of having breakfast in her robe and slippers. When she came back through the lobby, the young man at the desk buttonholed her to inform her of the hours that breakfast would be served in the lobby.

'I think I'm going to have it in my room,' she said.

'No problem,' the desk clerk said pleasantly. He asked her if she wanted a free newspaper delivered in the morning, and Eden gratefully agreed.

Just then a stout, gray-haired man in a plaid sport coat and a parka came up to the desk. 'Can I help you with those?' he asked, pointing to Eden's plastic bags bulging with water and crackers. 'I'm in the next suite over from yours.'

Eden leaned away from him, surprised and shocked as if she had been spied on, but the young clerk laughed.

'Don't mind Andy,' he said. 'He's here so much he thinks of this place as his neighborhood.'

'I do indeed, Oren.'

Eden smiled wanly. 'Oh, I see.'

Andy, undaunted by Eden's obvious discomfort, plucked one of the plastic sacs from her hands, and opened the door to the sidewalk. 'Shall we?' he said.

Eden wasn't quite sure how to act in the face of overbearing friendliness, but the clerk was looking at them with benign amusement. She walked along beside Andy, who explained that he was on the road and away from his beloved home in Indiana, his wife and children, for almost half the year. 'Counting the days till I retire,' he said as they reached their respective doors. 'Though to tell the truth, I'll probably miss the road.' He handed Eden back her bag with a smile. 'If you need anything now, Eden, I'm right next door.'

Eden thanked him, although she did not feel totally comfortable with his familiarity. 'Good night,' she said, and hurried to lock the door behind her.

The hours until the arranged meeting dragged, but at last it was time to get into her car and go. She left some extra time so she could negotiate her way across Cleveland, but, as she had six weeks earlier during the funeral visit, Eden found it an easy matter to get around. The city traffic was not the cutthroat affair that she was accustomed to in the New York area. People seemed to take their time, and there was usually a moment where one could peer at an address, or make a last-minute turn without the screeching of brakes all around.

They had agreed that Flynn would pick the restaurant for

their first editorial meeting, and Flynn had decided on an Italian restaurant called Alfredo's. Eden was picturing an old-world sort of place, with dim lights and candles, and a shiny mahogany bar. The reality was something very different. Eden parked her car on the busy, rundown block, and walked to the storefront with the striped awning which read Alfredo's. She went in and was greeted by a pot-bellied man in a black T-shirt, wearing an apron stained with red gravy. The restaurant was filled with Formica topped tables. There were napkin dispensers and shaker jars of Parmesan on every table.

'I'm meeting . . . um, Flynn Darby. He might have made a reservation,' she said.

But before the word was out of her mouth, the proprietor shook his head. 'Sit anywhere,' he said.

Eden went to a table against the wall near the back. Along the wall was a painted mural of someone's imagined version of the Amalfi coast, with stone buildings overlooking the sea from a verdant Italian hillside. That was about it for décor. The menus were laminated and almost as big as the tabletop. Eden picked one up and felt grease on her fingers.

The bell jingled on the front door and Eden looked up to see Flynn Darby entering the restaurant, carrying a bottle in a brown paper bag. For a moment she was able to study him before he noticed her. She hoped to banish that image of a drunken lout at his wife and son's funeral. But little had changed. He was undeniably good-looking, although his hair was, again, unkempt and his engineer boots were scuffed and unfastened. He was wearing a T-shirt that was frayed at the neck, under a battered leather jacket. He seemed lonely and forlorn, and he exuded a labile sexual energy. Eden immediately recalled that moment in his book when he first met her mother. He had described their encounter, from both their points of view. For his part, he had seen only Tara's aging, but still intense beauty. But he said that her first instinct toward him seemed to be almost motherly. She saw a bad boy in him, who needed protecting. Looking at him now, Eden could imagine it. Her mother had always been attracted to outsiders, to rebels. Sometimes Tara seemed to chafe at her comfortable life with Hugh, as if it did not reflect her authentic self. And everything about this man seemed to fairly scream danger. Whatever the magnetism had been which drew them together, their meeting was an instant of soulful recognition which could not be denied. For either one of them.

Flynn murmured to the proprietor, and then glanced to the back of the room and caught sight of Eden, seated beside the wall. He handed the paper bag to the proprietor, and came to join her.

'You found it, I see,' he said.

Eden looked around and nodded. 'You could have picked something a little more . . . luxurious. You do know the company's paying for this,' she said.

Flynn looked at her through heavy-lidded eyes, bemused. 'You don't like this place?' he asked, pulling out the chair across from her.

'No, it's fine,' she said.

'I like the food here,' said Flynn, sitting down heavily. 'Nothing pretentious.'

Eden nodded. 'Whatever you think.'

'What do you want?' he asked.

'Excuse me?' Eden asked, startled. 'What do you mean?'

'To eat. What do you want to eat?'

Eden felt flustered. 'I don't know. What do you recommend?'

'Everything's good,' said Flynn. He gestured to the proprietor, who arrived immediately at their table, holding the uncorked bottle of wine. Flynn looked over at Eden.

Eden ordered pasta and a salad.

'You're being overly cautious. You've got that New York superiority thing going on. But you may be surprised.'

Eden gazed back at him coolly. 'I'm not that hungry,' she said.

Flynn tipped his chair back and looked at her through narrowed eyes. 'I feel like I know you. From your mother,' he said.

Eden did not want to hear it. She decided to turn the tables. 'Do you like living here in Cleveland?' she said. 'Are you going to stay?'

'No,' he said bluntly. 'We only came here because of Dr Tanaka's work on Katz-Ellison syndrome. At that point, your mother was willing to try anything.'